PLUMPVILLE 2

$LUMPVILLE

2

It Is What It Is

Slumpville 2: It Is What It Is
© 2020 Wesley Bailey

Published by YDD Publishing

Cover Design: Trugfx

For more information on Wesley Bailey and/ or YDD Publishing, go to Ig: @Rapper_YDD or www.seriesbyydd.com

Library of Congress Cataloging-in Publication Data

IBSN: 978-1-7354607-2-7

Printed in the United States of America

PROLOGUE

"Yeah, nigga yeah!" ... There and alive was a nigga Young Dirty knew he had just killed the night before. He's had dreams of all the people he killed lately. And really, ever since his mother's funeral, doing it off and on. He woke up sweating, finding his .45 already in his hand with one in the head. Trina awoke out of her sleep and helped him take off his tank top. She been going through these occasions with him and had not once complained about her lack of sleep, her mind was focused on being there for her man.

"Bae you gonna shake that shit ... It just takes time," Trina was speaking from experience because she too had been through that process. When her brother was killed, she made a death storm go thorough Dade County until she got to the source. But after the revenge, all the deaths that lead to it came back every time she closed her eyes. And she lost weight and all while going through it.

"Baby, tomorrow me & brah going to Canada so I'll be gone for four days. Can you handle that or should I call Mook and leave him the pickup list?"

"I got chu bae, yo young ass betta enjoy yourself cause not everybody gets to go to Canada." She been holding Young Dirty down like a real thug misses and kinda wished she could go too. She never been out of the country and dreamed of going to Canada as a lil' girl. She understood his business and so she knew her place though.

"You be ready to leave since it sounds like you wanna go. I'm finna tell brah you coming. Be-Be coming too, I just ain't know how to ask you," as she smiled from ear to ear. This young nigga gonna fuck my world up she thought to herself. She loved the childish shy side he had; it was sexy to her.

" Let's celebrate our vacation," she said. She didn't wait for confirmation either. Before he could respond, his dick was down the back of her throat. He tensed up and curled his toes at the surprise sensation. Guiding with his hand, he took control of the head rotation while fingering and massaging her with his other hand. She was drenched as soon as he got there. The soft moan she let out let him know their feelings were mutual. She licked his nuts and sucked his dick with so much class, he felt like the king of the world. She rose and while he was still at attention and slowly slid down his pole backwards. After grabbing two hands full of ass, he started the ride to ecstasy. She was the first to buck but he wasn't far behind. He turned over while turning her with him and gave her all he had, beating the pussy from the back. He wanted her as a baby mama so shooting his kids in her was something he did ever since they started fucking, not knowing she was already pregnant.

After a shower and some designer clothes, he was in traffic. It was still early, 5:30 to be exact but collecting at a different time will throw niggas off that was watching all the time. After the death of his mama, he went headfirst in da streets and said fuck the rap. He still did features when asked to represent Florida, but his mind was too far gone for the rap games and he vowed to die in da streets like his mother did.

"Yo Peanut...." Peanut was half woke half sleep but still at the trap.

"What's good nephew?" He got out early by taking classes that Fat Rat felt was unnecessary and been back at it like he never left.

"I'm finna pull up, you ready?"

"I like how you move youngin', I'm waiting on you."

"Say No Mo!" Young Dirty ended the call and turned on Jefferson Drive. Peanut had relocated and where he stayed the street was like a horseshoe, so he seen everything with his spot being right in the middle of it. He was waiting with a duffle bag when Young Dirty turned in. Once in the back seat, he swapped identical bags and made conversation on some being safe shit.

"Y'all going kangaroo riding aint'a?" He knew it should be close to that time cause he been pushing green too lately. With the price they was giving it to him for he couldn't say no.

"We'll be back on schedule by Monday but I got fifty if you need it."

"I'll hold off but make a nigga number one cause sometimes Monday mean next Friday." They both laughed as Peanut exited the vehicle. Once he backed out he was headed to Grant Side to holla at Gally Gal. Ever since his momma passed and he learned she was there last, it was where he went often to kick it.

"Come on in jitt and fye up some of that shit I smell in yo pocket," Gally Gal represented for the females of Slumpville. She was always with the movement whether it involved babysitting or setting fuck niggas up to be killed. He and Shay went way back and although Dirty never spent this much time over here with her before his momma death. He could see why she did, they were just alike.

"You know Red Clid coming home next month. I'ma call you when it get close so you could put in towards the block party for 'em," Young Dirty sat down at the dining room table, pulled out a bag of pressure then went back in his pocket and pulled out a wad of hundreds.

"I been moving so fast that I ain't even sent dawg nothing lately either so hunh," He handed Gally Gal $2,500 and busted open a swisha.

"You get five and the rest for him and the party. Don't let me miss it. I'ma take 'em shopping too, so let me know when he jump." Red Clid was from the generation before his, so he grew up looking up to him and seen him as a big brother in the game. He spent an hour smoking and kicking da shit with Gally Gal then left. His phone went off while driving and his day started.

"Yo....."

"Blood this Mook, I'm at Ric spot. Somebody just killed Toon my nigga. They killed 'em and I always thought the nigga couldn't die." Dirty had the car music up he was bumping completely down now.

"Where you at? He there?"

"Yeah blood but he gone. Don't worry tho the nigga that killed 'em here to and he finna die." Young Dirty heard the shots go off

"POP, POP, POP"

"Blood, we goin need a new doctor cause Ric ain't gone be able to help nobody else."......

TABLE OF CONTENTS

CHAPTER 1

Boo was sitting at the bar at *Bosses Only*, the restaurant Shay and the other women of the family had opened up when he noticed a Mexican walking towards him staggering. He could tell that that Mexican wasn't average by the one hundred-thousand-dollar watch, it happened to be the same watch he had on. His street instincts kicked in and he headed behind the Mexican trying to catch up to him. He followed behind, but at a 15 to 20-foot radius which is why the two car thieves didn't see him. By the time the Mexican unlocked his door, they were on him. One boy choked the Mexican who was pissy drunk and the other started going through his pockets. By the time they both looked, two twin Rugers were pointed at both of 'em.

"Can I help you broke mothafuckas?" Boo had murda on his mind and really didn't know if he was helping the Mexican or just mad they beat him to the lick.

"Ain't no problem," the one that was choking him said as he let the Mexican go as they backed away wishing they were strapped. The Mexican was speaking Spanish but Boo knew enough to decipher that he was mad about what happened.

"I don't know you but I do know you too drunk to drive" Boo said. The Mexican was getting off the ground from being released by the dude that was choking him and looking at his outfit.

"You drive!" He said to Boo with a swagger that showed who's boss. He then walked over the passenger side and got in so Boo could take the wheel. Once in the car Boo asked, "Where do you live?"

"Marriott, top floor. I have a room," He answered drunkenly. The migo was asleep before they made it to the light. Boo was asking himself, *what the fuck am I doing.* He was taking a chance and prayed it paid off because the real Boo would wack the Mexican and take everything but his drawers. They pulled up to the Marriott and woke him up.

"Aye homie, What's your name?"

"Carlos. We there?" Boo locked at the Migo and how cool he was about the current situation and had to smile. This Mexican think he untouchable he said to himself.

"Yeah, we here."

"Well come in and have a drink with me. I'll have a driver take you back to the restaurant later." Boo thought Carlos was still just drunk talking bout a driver and only agreed to go in because he was hoping to find some money or dope to make all this shit worth it. After entering the making lobby, three muscular Mexicans dressed in all black tuxedos walked up quickly and the one in the middle spoke fast and heatedly.

"You no call, you leave with no one. You tell me no one, fuck you doing boss!" Him questioning his boss only made Carlos mad because as far as he knew he was grown. He had left unknowingly because he was upset about losing a shipment and needed a drink or two. Without a warning he slapped the shit out the Mexican that questioned him.

"You work for me Punto!" He kicked him in the stomach as he laid on the floor in the middle of the lobby and walked off as if nothing ever happened. Boo was at a loss for words. He followed behind Carlos until they made it to the elevator where Carlos had to put in a key in order to go to his room. When the elevator opened, they were in the front room of the suite. Boo knew he was fucking with a boss because there were at least four more Mexicans dressed the same way in the suite with A.R. 15's and that alone made Boo uncomfortable even though he was strapped.

"What do you do for a living?" Carlos asked as he went behind the wet bar and started fixing two drinks.
"I supply and demand. My family owns the restaurant you was at thanks to our real family business," Boo didn't know if he was saying too much but he didn't want to *not* say enough if this turned into an opportunity. Carlos was thinking about the loss he just took.

"Show me something..." Boo was confused now so he asked, "Show you what?"

"Show me your loyalty and I promise to beat any number you're paying. I want them two mothafuckas that tried to rob me dead tomorrow. I want to read about them in tomorrow's paper. You do that and I'll front you as much as you can handle."

3

"Say No Mo." Boo headed for the door determined to handle business and do his part towards helping the family. He knew his clique will find anybody if that mothafucka violated. He was on his phone walking out of the lobby of the hotel when a black four door Audi pulled up with black tints and he went fo his straps when the windows started letting down. One Mexican that was there when the other one got slapped was in the driver seat and said, "Where to?" The next morning when Carlos got the morning paper, it read "*Two Black Males Were Gunned Down in the Parking Lot of Bosses Only Restaurant,*" and he knew who did it. From that point on Boo was plugged in. They even started serving Luciano work because the ticket they were giving him was three grand short of what he was already paying.....

CHAPTER 2

"Here, get this shit!" Ms. Mac Clain handed Bobby Joe, one of Fat Rat workers, a pack containing four zips of pressure, two cans of bulgar's, and three touch screens.

"Say lil' mama, I'm just asking but how much homez paying you cause I think I could do better." She looked at Bobby Joe as if he had to be crazy to ask or say that which he had to be because if Fat Rat knew, she could only imagine.

"You got a position nigga, so play it," was all she said before walking back in the booth that watched over the federal dorms. The text she sent Fat Rat had him already prepared to deal with Bobby Joe as he stepped in the room. Mike-Mike from Leesburg was there too. So was lil Puff, Snowman, and Veg. Bobby Joe put the pack on the desk in the room as if it was his pack and he was breaking bread. With no questions asked Mike-Mike went into action, slapping the shit outta Bobby Joe and knocking him on the desk. He pulled out his 8-inch banger that he just made that morning and was dying to use it and went to work. Like Ms. Mac Clain said, everybody had a position to play and Mike them was goons and killas. Veg had Bobby tied and gagged and recorded Speed as they took turns stabbing and taking pictures of Bobby, then sending them to different camps with the message, "Disloyalty leads to this" being sent with them. Once Fat Rat thought it was enough and he knew fa sho that Bobby was dead, he told them to clean up and started bussin' down the pack. He had four months to go and couldn't wait to be back around niggas he knew he wouldn't have to question when it came to loyalty or keeping it a hunnit. A text went to his phone and after reading it he had to laugh at Ms. Mac Clain, saying that she love him and he could do way better than his baby mama. No one could ever top Shonta and her comparing herself to somebody she didn't even know told Fat Rat that she wasn't bossed up enough for his speed which he already knew. He simply responded, "Check..." and cut his phone off. He just wanted to get high and pretend he was back out in da streets of Slumpville. He heard Red Clid was coming home, Spook got out, Lover and Zink too. He knew when he finally did get out, the hood was gone be swole and that thought alone allowed him to block out the fact his young niggas was chopping Bobby Joe in pieces and flushing him down the hard pressure metal toilet. The over crowed population allowed shit like that to happen and fuck niggaz allowed it to happen to them.

****

"When I bent da corner, this nigga had his dick down Ty Ty throat like she was his bitch and not a crack head." Hearing Lil Rat tell how he seen him getting head from a basa forced Koko to do nothing but laugh at being

6

caught. He wasn't embarrassed because every dope boy or street boy done had they time of tricking off with a crackhead. Some of the best head and pussy came from a bitch that smoke dope.

"I had to see why they call her good head red," Koko said while still laughing. Koko went to school with Lil Rat in elementary and always kicking it with 'em in the hood but since becoming a member of D.B.M.G (Dope Boy Muscle Gang), he spent almost every day around his ex-school mate. When Young Dirty lost his mama, he had three bodies put under his belt and the money he was making at his young age was a plus.

"Y'all niggas hold it down while I'm gone and be ready when I get back," Lil Rat told his crew of young niggas.

"Nigga I'm ready now," said Drama which was the newest of the click and the wildest.

"You just be ready when you get back cause you know the festival coming up in Hustleville and I'ma act a ass, D.B.M.G style." They all started dappin' each other up talking about how they gone turn up in their rivalry hood. Through the years, D.B.M.G made a name for themselves and after the murder spree, they fell back trying not to draw heat and be taken off the streets. One thing that was fa sho though, if you fuck with them, you gone make the news- Dead or missing.......

J-Lee was the only one with a loud spot in Tavares because not too many niggas hustle close to the county jail and the county jail wasn't nothing but a skip and a hop from the hood in Tavares. He sucked up plenty paper being that the first thing a mothafucka want once released is some gas to get high. He started sending bags to his mob brothers in Atlanta for a player ticket and kept Montiano with reefer although he was in Spalding County waiting in his new trial. The layer had just gotten another hunnit thousand towards the case and appeal so $400 thousand was keeping him there with faith to walk. J-Lee peaked through the blinds. He was wide awake at 4:13 a.m. thanks to the pure coke he was getting from Lil Rat them. He would jug a few birds to some niggas in some of the local areas, but not before taking out a zip or two for his personal consumption and replacing it with baking soda the re-rocking it and still having good dope. No one knew that he did coke and no one questioned it so he didn't volunteer the information. It was day three with no sleep or a full meal, but the room full of shoe boxes stuffed with money made it all in a day's work. Literally......

CHAPTER 3

My dawg just got killed,

His daughter miss him a lot.

Mama prayed for a change and voted for Rick Scott.

My nigga was on some otha shit,

Doop boys kicked in his door one afternoon...

Caught 'em wit a brick and a broom stick.

Tha whole hood made cause jitt had the whole hood rich.

Like fuck a drought, Jitt on some all the time

All good shit....."

Mook boy spit bar after bar to a sold-out crowd at a club in Orlando called Hero's. He had everybody rappin' along with him and a D.B.M.G promotion group of females in the crowd selling his C.D's to the ones that didn't have it or just wanted to holla. After the song, he gave a shout out to his only real close friend Toon. Drunk, high off mango kush, and feeling good, he walked off stage still in his feelings about his lost partner and didn't see it coming.

"POP! POP! POP!" Everybody got low and scattered. Females was yelling and niggas was searching for who they came with. Mook Boy laid on the ground with three to the chest still looking at the shooter.

"Die slow fuck nigga, tell Toon I said fuck 'em." After speaking his peace, he blended in with the crowd and fled.

Mook Boy was now not only glad he had his vest on, but now he knew who shot Toon...... His Cousin.....

****

Destiny's! Shonta read her sew in hair salon name out loud before walking into her place of business.

"Girl bring her here," Blackberry reached out and grabbed Destiny out of her mother's arms.

"How's Auntie baby," Destiny was stirring out her sleep and smiled at the sight of her favorite Auntie. Blackberry let Destiny down after kissing her cheek and said, "You want auntie to do your hair?"

"Yes ma'am," Destiny said excitedly and jumped in her chair ready to play Barbie. Shonta and Samantha had three hair salons, two nail salons, and a clothing store in the Lake Square Mall on Hwy 441 which brought in the biggest profit due to only selling high end and designer clothing. They always had celebrities coming through to shop when they were in the area compliments of Mr. Fat Rat. Her and Blackberry were in a conversation about the clothing store when Shonta glanced at the news playing on the tv on the wall and seen a picture of Mook Boy.

"Cut that up!" She prayed he ain't go to jail or killed nobody. She had already heard about Ric and Toon.

"... At a rapper concert he became a target. Reports say the rapper was shot repeatedly before the suspect disappeared in a crowd of fans that came to watch the rapper perform. The conditions do the rapper is still unknown." Shonta was already on the phone calling Mook Boy and hoping he answered himself because she didn't want to hear any more bad news, she had her fair share over the years.

"You have reached the voicemail box of 407-84..." she hung up and dialed again.

****

"Bae look at this shit," Trina was excited and couldn't hide her childhood thrill to be at the top of the globe. As both couples exited the airport door, they seen two black on black Tahoe's headed in their direction. Big Ock right hand man Kimpo got out the back seat of the first vehicle, after this 6-foot 10 African warrior opened it and stood aside.

"Peace," he said to both Lil Rat and Young Dirty.

"Love," they both responded taking turns shaking hands and headed to their African plug.

"We flew in early like you said but I ain't going to lie big homie, I hate surprises so please tell me the news he wanted to tell us," Young Dirty said once seated in the back along with Kimpo and Lil Rat. The ladies were placed in the other vehicle so the men could discuss business but was promised a night and time they would remember.

"Patience lil' nigga, he ain't got nothing to tell you, it's what he got to show you that might change yo life." With both brothers being in the presence of a boss, they knew it was something worth shutting the fuck up and riding for so Young Dirty sat back and began rolling from the pound of C.F., Canada's finest that was on the built-in table inside the Tahoe. The vehicles separated with the ladies going to the hotel and the men headed to handle business. Forty-five minutes, later they were riding through the forest like woods on a road that looked like it lead to the middle of nowhere then the Tahoe took a sharp turn off the road through a path that wasn't visible to non-users. After another five minutes they pulled next to a truck that looked as if it was monitoring the half of mountain in view, full of plants and workers. Once the vehicle completely stopped, Big Ock got in letting them take in the site then said, "It's 250 acres. A friend of mine built this with blood, sweat and tears. His wife's the head Mounty here and she gets a percentage. I'm telling you this because not long ago my friend passed away and left this to me. Without him, I have no business here. I'm going back home to the motherland where I'm opening up my forth casino and resort." Big Ock was looking out the window thinking about the times him and his dear friend had been coming to Canada from Africa and starting a business that made both of them millionaires. Once his friend met Sarah and she planted the idea of growing with her helping, the vacation turn into a stay.

"I'm leaving the crew that's been running thing so everything should still go smooth but make sure Sarah get her percentage because I promised her she'll be straight and I meant it." He was looking at them now with a no bullshit tone in his voice. All Lil Rat could do is look at Young Dirty and say, "We goin fuck the city up!..."

CHAPTER 4

"Fuck nigga where it's at," Boo was mad as a mothafucka that Ju-Ju actually tried to steal from him. He brought Ju-Ju to the circle thinking he had what it takes but he really had a different kind of take in mind.

"Please don't kill me man I had to," Boo was enraged just from hearing him confess to stealing the three grand that was missing out if the ninety-eight thousand he came to pick up from him Lil' Drop, his big homie from Apopka. Even though three-grand wasn't shit to Boo, it was the fact Ju-Ju thought shit was sweet that made him slap the shit out of 'em again with his pistol.

"Who made you do it pussy?" All Boo saw was murder and the thought of somebody testing him was the initiation of death to that individual.

"Cat Daddy," Man said he ran shit now and if I didn't give him a percentage, he was going to kill my lil girl. She all I- POP! POP!" ..... Two shots ended Ju-Ju's life and he slumped over still chained to the light pole dead in the hood for everybody to see. Boo was making a statement and everybody got the picture loud and clear.... Cat Daddy was the leader of a crew called Cats and Dawgs. They was making a lil' noise but couldn't to compare to what D.B.M.G was becoming. Boo walked to his R8 Audi with one thing on his mind....Murder.

****

Cat Daddy was counting his first one hundred grand when his phone rang, "Talk." It was his soldier Lil' Dee and fear the sound of his voice, it wasn't good.

"Dawg dead and tied to the light pole out here. They say he told Boo bout the money we been getting and Boo offed 'em. It's war time for real now my nigga and we can't half step."

"TAT, TAT, TAT, TAT, TAT, TAT! Drama's Yappa cut Lil Dee conversation short and ripped him in half.

"DEE!" Cat Daddy yelled in the phone after hearing the gun shots. He didn't receive a response so he knew his partner was dead. He was finna hang up when he heard a voice speak thru the line.

"You next," was all that he said before the line went dead. The war was officially on and so far D.B.M.G was winning.....

****

"Say blood, I know what I saw. Fuck you think I'm doing lying?!" Mook Boy was 38 hot that his Uncle King Lo didn't believe that his son and Mook Boy cousin, Cat Daddy, tried to take Mook boy life.

15

"Nephew I'm not saying shit, but for you to know 100% that that's what you saw, this shit sound crazy as a mothafucka though. Between me and you, growing up Cat Daddy looked up to you and I believe you already know that shit," King Lo said before taking another puff of da blunt Mook Boy brought for them to burn and let him fire up out of respect. The effect of the reefa hit him quickly and he was dumb high but the feeling continued to get stronger and stronger and for some reason, Mook Boy didn't hit it once it was passed to him. That's when it really hit 'em.

"Nephew what the hell kinda-aghhh," King Lo brain felt as if it was boiling and his lungs shut down with smoke still inside so breathing was impossible.

"Tell your pussy ass son when he join you that he did this shit to you," Mook Boy said with no love in his heart and walked out his Uncle spot knowing King Lo will be dead before he made it to the car. He loved his uncle and cousin but when it came to the murder attempt on his life and he heard him speak about Toon, then everything Cat Daddy love became a target including his own family.

"Auntie where you at?...... Well I'm on my way I got to talk to you about this baby momma of mine.... I just was with Cat last night.... Alright I'll be there in 20 minutes." Mook Boy hung up headed to kill his favorite Auntie and didn't think twice about what he did or was finna do because when he lost Toon, he lost his morals. Now slump

16

or get slumped is a motto everybody around him need to think about because if he seen any shade in you, then you going to join his Uncle and Lord knows what's going to happen to Cat Daddy, but first he finna make him suffer like he did when he lost Toon but worse.......

CHAPTER 5

"I'm Da Baddest Bitch.... Da Baddest Bitch," Shay was riding through Carver Heights in Leesburg playing her son new girlfriend song and singing along like she wrote it. No one knew Shay was alive and it killed her to fake her own death to her sons, Lil Rat and Young Dirty, but she had her reasons. She was a true vet and knew her role and would do whatever it took to see her family prosper because she'll never forget the cold, lonely, and hungry days her and jitt been thru. A wise man use to stress that the most dangerous thing in life is the unknown. With that in her head she pulled up to where Cat Daddy was hiding on Mis-Pa Ave. She had been looking and buying information on his whereabouts since Mook Boy concert. She was the one who sent the unknown text from the throwaway phone about Lil' Dee being out there where Boo left Ju-Ju. Now she was at Cat Daddy's duck off because she always loved finishing unfinished business. She knew by how she was finna do Cat Daddy that once her son hear about it, he'll know she still alive without anyone else knowing. He made it rain bullets after her death and she really as happy at the test she put him through and how she *did* find the mothafucka who attempted to kill her. That's what let her know she was ready to do it on his own. From the looks of the spot where Cat Daddy was at, you'll think no one stayed there in years but the light that was on last night

when she rode by gave 'em away. She loaded her twin Glock 9's, both with .45 round extendos, and placed silencers on them too. Halfway to then door she noticed the blinds move. She didn't flinch at all. The UPS uniform and logo on her rental gave her permission to have the wrong address.

"Yes may I help you?" a young female who look no older than 18 answered the door, half-naked and half-awake. But the chrome pink twins woke her up completely though the fifth shot put her back to sleep forever. Shay stepped over her just in time to see Cat Daddy reaching for his own Glock 9.

"Touch it and make the news fuck nigga!" He froze knowing this type of shit was out his league... When he decided to start beef, he didn't think shit would go to the level it did. He was used to "hood beefing," mean mugging and even club fighting or hood shootouts but D.B.M.G was on some real mob shit and he was nowhere near their level. Only his hatred for his cousin Mook Boy for not putting him down motivated him to start his own click and the news he got this morning about his father proved that his cousins was after him too. He felt his eyes was playing tricks on him once he took a good look at his assassin.

"Shay?... You dead... You!"

"Shut da fuck up! I do the talking mothafucka. You think you can fuck wit us?! Bitch we do this shit for real, you insulted us by shooting Mook cause real gangstas don't die, can't you see dat?" She was up on him now and her twins were so deep in his skin he knew if he tried anything he was shot... Repeatedly.

"Sit down fuck nigga," she kicked him onto the couch with her $900 red bottoms. "I'ma make an example outta you." She then reached in the box that was in her hand when she was at the door and pulled out and unfolded a Choppa right in front of his face.

"The clip got 50 in it. You could get the whole 50 if you don't act right," she had his full attention because he did not want to die and the bitch he brought home last night proved to him that Shay would kill something. She pulled out a piece of paper and a pen (red ink) and gave him instructions. Once he did as he was told, she still gave him the whole 50. The bag she taped to it caught every shell she spit at 'em, so all she had to do was grab her box and walk back out like she came. She knew that news about no shells being found would grab her sons attention because it was his signature move but there was no doubt in her mind the note left would tell it all. Once down the road from the crime scene still listening to Trina, she pulled out a throw away phone and texted, "Cat Daddy dead, watch da news," to Boo phone then threw the phone out the window.....

CHAPTER 6

"Bae my next video goin' to be here, this shit is to die for," Trina was talking with excitement and had been since Young Dirty walked through the door. They had been out sight-seeing, visited the Zoo and shopped like it was going outta style. They ran into a couple of celebrities and to Trina surprise, a lot of females knew who she was.

"I don't want to leave yet either, I wish we could move out here away from everybody back home," she said seriously. Young Dirty flopped down on the bed and laid back. He had enjoyed every second he was there simply because it made Trina happy, but he was ready to get back home and get shit poppin'. Boo had been keeping him updated on everything that was going on and to see the problem handled on such short notice made him smile and feel good about his team. The situation about Cat Daddy made the news so Young Dirty pulled out his iPhone and pulled it up on YouTube. Once the video was over he was left stunned. He had a signature style of wackin' and this way of killing caught his attention. He got thrills off other people that think like him so he noted to get a few more details about his death to see who knocked him off. Trina didn't know how much her every wish could be granted because if business go as planned they could end up moving to the North Pole like she dreamed.

21

"Let's just enjoy our stay now and live life Lil' Mama. Come show me what those African women was showing you in yoga today." She blushed and came to her king feeling like a teenage lover with her teenage boyfriend of hers.

"You know, I think we love yo young ass," she said smartly.

"You betta love my young ass," Young Dirty said back not catching on before kissing her passionately and pulling her on top of him. Controlling her body weight by her thighs, he turned over with her and started planting kisses working his way down to her love box. He stopped at her left nipple and took in a mouth full of her. She inhaled deeply and gave him more of her as her nipple hardened and her hormones jumped. Taking turns going from one breast to the other only complemented the fact that he was two fingers deep in her pinkness. He used this thumb to massage her clit and with her eyes in the back of her head, she exploded shivering, while gripping the headboard.

"That's one," Young Dirty whispered before going for round two by replacing his finger with something longer and wider. She came two more times before he did and they both went to sleep in their own world. She whispered in his ear while he was halfway resting, "I'm pregnant..."

****

"Ty, you really think this shit goin' to work?" Samantha found herself pregnant but in Hustleville with Tyiesha and Mesha plotting on a way to get Cat Daddy to come out of hiding.

"Bitch I fucked the nigga twice and both times it was this that got his ass over here." They were referring to the pictures of them naked with each other as if they were fucking. The situation had Samantha thinking 'bout Shay, her favorite cousin and how they did something similar to that fetish wise when they got Puncho and Shay killed him. Remembering the gangsta in her cousin made her smile and seconds after reminiscing her phone went off. The number was unknown but her mind said to answer it which is something she didn't normally do.

"Who diz?" she said with an attitude.

"Cat Daddy dead and leave them hoes alone!" The phone line went dead after those words was spoken and Samantha didn't know whether to be shocked, sad, cry, happy, scared, or what. She did know that voice from anywhere in the world but she didn't think anybody would believe her. Hell, she was wondering if it was true that Shay just chastised her from the grave.......

****

Shay deleted the pictures out of Cat Daddy phone that Samantha them sent and threw it in the trash can along with the phone she called on before boarding her plane. She stopped short when she seen her son coming from off a plane with Trina, Lil Rat, and Be-Be. She smiled at how big and grown both of her babies were and she also thought about Boo and Mook Boy. They team was solid and she wanted so badly to go and hug both of 'em and never call Samantha back, but she had to check herself. Her work wasn't done and thanks to Luciano she'll have to stay hiding there until they capture and kill the mothafucka that's tryna put all of them in the feds forever, thinking Puncho worked for the feds and they supplied him with good weed to set niggas up. And to top it off, the whole killing and robbery was caught on camera planted in his house by the feds. Now with the feds on their trails and with her being the shooter, she had to fake her death to get the feds to fall back enough so she could fix the situation. She had already killed the two officers assigned to watch and take pictures of her some them leaving the airport. Joe she was headed to see Luciano about the info he had that would clear her for good. She still had a few more years before she could come out of hiding for faking her death, but she'll no longer have to not communicate with her family. A single tear fell from her eyes and she boarded her plane unseen.

CHAPTER 7

Fuck nigga tried 2 off me, do me sum bad,

Now the streets saying, I always get the last laugh.

In blowing mango getting head from his baby mama,

Me and Drama ran a train, yeah dats my young gunna.

Try me, bitch you use to be me young runna,

Everybody play position, you didn't respect honor.

Mook was still hot even after hearing of the death of his cousin who tried to end his life. Only people that was close knew they were cousins, and that not only did Cat Daddy make the news but his shooter, mama, daddy, and baby mama did too.

Real niggaz live, fuck niggas die quick

What you say hunh, wat you say,

Can't hear nothin' from a dead bitch.

He was reckless with no limits, I thought he signed with P.

His death ticket was signed, by yours truly me!

The crowd went ape shit and everybody that knew who he was talking bout had all the rumors they heard confirmed. Mook Boy been gangsta but the way he handled Cat Daddy took his street cred to another level. Most of the club had red flags and his music inspired young niggas to join that Blood gang shit, niggas and bitches paid respect to him in the V.I.P. after his show. He had his shirt off with no vest to get his point across that he ain't worried 'bout no fuck nigga. Jeezy had asked if they could do a song together and he a Crip. Real recognize real which is why all street niggas that had become celebrities, started taking Mook seriously and wanted to fuck wit 'em. When you talking 'bout how gangsta you are, it's good to have REAL gangstas somewhere and Mook Boy was one. He had started blowing up world-wide and doing shows in New York, Detroit, Texas, and sold out Canada where a lot street niggas retired to. He also was moving more dope than planned thanks to the dumb low ticket he was paying Lil' Rat them and how quickly the real dope boys that come to his shows always wanna shop. He made his first half a million off the streets and off the music industry at the same time then, making him a millionaire. D.B.M.G was more known then Trill Ent. or Cash Money Records. Fat was coming home tomorrow and he already knew Fat had a planned to get the gawp and he was down. After the show as he was walking to his corvette he drove to the show in Ocala and could've sworn he seen Shay. He chalked it up as a memory and said, "God bless her" to himself in a whisper out of respect and went home....

Once he made it to his castle he already had one in the head of his Ruger and murder on his mind. He knew fa sho that the black Buick Lacrosse that followed him for the last five blocks using the same tactics he did, so he knew what was up. Walking to his doorstep wondering if he was just drunk or finna body a mothafucka had him feeling like he was in a gangsta movie and the gas in his system made him smile at that thought.

"What's so funny?" He knew that voice so before turning around he said, "I'm laughing at how gangsta shit be every time you sound and how I didn't believe you was dead in the first place. Real gangstas don't die." He faced Shay and seen her leaning against his shit blowing on mango which was his favorite kind of gas.

"Two gangstas, two murder attempts, nobody dies. I think we made for each other," Mook Boy wasn't shocked to see Shay. He was the normal Mook Boy towards her and she smiled at the embrace.

"One labor, two sons, a million rounds. I think my hands full. ...And Cat Daddy left you this," she handed him a note written in red ink with blood drops on it that said *Disloyalty is unforgivable and family first.* Mook Boy read it and then said, "You still putting in work even after your death." Shay smiled at his comment. Mook Boy was a real gangsta and his sauce always grabbed females attention. He was smooth but dangerous and if Shay didn't leave soon she might start taking him seriously.

"Let my kids read it. But don't tell them you seen me," her authority was the most sexiest thing about her to Mook. She was every bit of a dime, so to act and carry herself the way she did was rare.

28

"I got you Lil' mama and check on a nigga every now and then"

"I always keep you in my eyesight. You family and family first." Mook Boy looked at her in her eyes and said with sincerity, "Family First." D.B.M.G was his new family and she just showed him how serious she takes family matters by wackin' Cat Daddy herself. They hugged and she walked and got in her Buick. She knew the note would be a big deal to Young Dirty and prayed Mook Boy continued to keep it a hunnit with her about who she was or that she was back in tha city.....

CHAPTER 8

My life like a movie, my bitch looking groovy,

Maybe it's the weed

But I think she wanna screw me.

Lil' Rat was hitting a few bars he came up with to Be-Be who was living with him since they met four and a half months ago. He spent all his free time either at home with her or taking her somewhere. They went to Detroit a few times and each time Lil' Rat would spend a lil' time tryna link up with his partna Slick but it was nearly impossible being that Slick had his number changed. Lil' Rat found it strange that Slick changed numbers but didn't give it to him and hoped ain't nothing happened to his friend. Him and Be-Be where at the food court in Lake Square Mall after a shopping spree.

"Don't tell nobody I'm tryna rap either cause that'll be lame"

" I won't but I don't think it'll be lame; I think you should tell your father." Lil' Rat looked her in the eyes and showed her a site of concern then said, "What about your father?" she was caught off guard. "You never speak on your father and mother or the relationship y'all have," he continued. "I want to know everything about you so please don't leave me out." She sat quiet for a minute thinking of the right words if there were any.

30

"Me and my father don't speak any more," she said with a little regret in her words. Lil' Rat could tell this was a tough conversation but when he saw her picture on Big Ock desk, all kinds of question started popping up. He even wondered if Big Ock knew he was coupled up with his daughter. Be-Be continued on.

"We were the perfect family til it happened.

"What happened?" Lil' Rat asked.

"Til he killed her after she was caught with his friend. My mother fell in love with two different people and as a child even though I know who my father was, I also knew that man that be with my father too. She would be with both friends and never got caught by my father. Then one year ago, mom and Ya-Ya which was his friend, were off creeping and the next day they both were found dead by multiple gun shots. I knew my father was behind it and I knew why. I just wanted to get away which is why I came down here to Florida and then I heard he was locked up for her death. Then I heard how he basically bought the case out because the only thing he went to a federal prison for was tax invasion and no murder. I still haven't seen him but recently heard he had gotten out." Be-Be was wiping her tears now that she got it out. She had been carrying her family situation on her shoulders and often had thoughts of going back to Canada, so when Lil' Rat said they were going, she had to mentally prepare. He never noticed how familiar she was, so fast to the roads and streets. She even went by her old place of residence on one of her runs but no one lived there anymore.

"How do you feel about yo pops?" Lil' Rat was tryna see if her love for her pops was still there after killing her mother. He never told her about seeing her picture and wanted them to bump heads in Canada, but Big Ock didn't pick them up from the airport. She thought for a minute again then said, "I wish no bad in him, I know he did it outta love and rage. I just needed some time away." Lil' Rat stood up and grabbed their bags, then grabbed her hand.

"Let's get outta here Lil' mama and listen to me. Tell him you're pregnant and not just gaining weight on me." She had a look of surprise in her face now.

"How did you know?" She asked shocked, not knowing how to tell Lil' Rat bout being pregnant.

"I notice everything about you. You're perfect to me and no matter if your gaining weight I'ma still see you as all I'll ever want but if you're pregnant, that would call for a celebration."

"Well yes, I'm pregnant!" She said excitedly because she didn't think Lil' Rat would want to keep it. They walked outside to the parking lot and once they were getting in the car he said to Be-Be, "Thank you Lil' mama." She just blushed.

"I'm serious, this shit we doing is new to me but I'm ready to be a man. Not just a man but I'm your man.

****

"Man Lisa, baby don't start!" Lisa baby looked at the phone with a stank face as if she was looking at who she was on the phone with.

"Slick these niggas ain't playing out here. They for real and if I'm not mistaken, they your family. You up and leave me saying you're going to Detroit and now you saying you're in protective custody and testifying against everybody in the hood we both grew up with, Like I'm supposed to be cool with dat shit... YOU PUSSY! Lose my number. The only reason why I won't tell Lil' Rat them is cause I love yo snitchin' ass but I can't respect how you live cuz that ain't Slumpville." And with that being said, Lisa Baby ended the call. Slick was left still holding the pay phone he snuck outside and got a feeling as if his world was crumbling. He came up to Detroit to flawse on some of his family members and catch a play for twelve bricks. The twelve-brick play was to an undercover and now with facing the rest of his life locked up, Slick chose to snitch. He only lived by the *DON'T SNITCH* concept because he never thought he'd be the one out under that pressure and now that he was, that concept was out the window. "Fuck her," he said to himself then headed back to the hotel he was hiding at while the feds checked out all the info on the Family First Mafia, as the feds named and gathered more evidence against them. He had love for the family but he had experienced a level in tha game that he just wasn't ready to leave. He figured once he testified, he'll just set up shop in Detroit and still be da kingpin. He knew he went out like a sack but he had other shit in life he could think about besides the fact.......

CHAPTER 9

Fat Rat was released and walked out of the prison gates in a $7,800 Steve Harvey edition three-piece suit. The $1,200 red bottoms he sported complement it the Phantom he walked up to. Red Clid was the first to get out, then Lil' Rat and Young Dirty was next.

"Say Unk, this shit feel good don't it!" Him and Red Clid embraced and he replied, "Fuck yeah, where da weed at and where Shonta? I'm tryna go home." They all got in the back with Lil' Rat and Red Clid facing Young Dirty. Red Clid pulled out a C.F. and started breaking down a swisha. He told Fat Rat, "I been out three months and still feel like I just left." Fat Rat agreed. He felt fresh just being able to do small shit like drive or roll a window down.

"What's on the agenda Lil niggas," he dapped both his sons up and the conversation turned to business.

"The numbers gonna have you smiling like a mothafucka. Luciano grabbing two thousand bricks a month and his paper always on point. We produce eleven hundred pounds a week, plus Mook Boy getting four to five hundred of 'em every two weeks, so we got over thirty mil saved up and don't really know what to do but hustle. The shops clean some, but we need more money cleaned and some overseas accounts. This briefcase is a mill in cash. This for you too, jewelry and suit shop and to get your shoe game up." After Young Dirty told him that, he lifted up his

35

foot to show his $6,500 Gucci Loafers. Lil' Rat lifted his foot and showed his $5,200 Louis Vuitton, gator trimmed loafers and they all started laughing.

"How much money you got Red Clid?"

"Bout 3.5, why what's up?"

"Because I love you my niggas and I wanted to make sho you straight." They dapped up again and started poppin bottles and blowing pressure. The life they were living was new to Fat Rat but he was adapting fast. They pulled up to a gated mansion and the driver put in a code before the gates opened up to allow them to proceed.

"This some Scarface type shit and a long way from da hood," Fat Rat was taking to everybody but mainly to himself.

"You ain't seen nothing yet," Lil' Rat said. "Yesterday I was on T.M.Z ballin in the club with Rick Ross and they all was talking 'bout how they heard the guy with Rick Ross had a million-dollar chain on." Fat Rat looked at Lil' Rat.

"Did you?" He asked surprised.

"Hell yeah. We got too much money pops. Now I'm known worldwide as the million-dollar chain man." Everybody laughed but Fat Rat.

"Fuck celebrating, our meeting will be in about three hours, so get everybody together and get rid of dat chain lil nigga before we all be in the feds." Fat Rat exited the vehicle and instead of going in the house he walked into the garage that had six cars and had six cars in it which each costed more than $100,000 apiece. During Fat Rat stay in prison he talked to and met a lot of different people that help sharpening his tools for life and most importantly, staying out of the feds. Deep inside Fat Rat knew that although his two boys was holding it down but as he walked through the garage with his briefcase, he knew it was a good chance the feds knew it too. He took a seat on one of the white leather chairs and opened the briefcase. All he seen was blue hunnits. The six hundred, thirty-four grand he had stashed for hard times was still buried in Slumpville at Ms. San house, who was the mother of the hood. As the head of the round table, he had not only a lot of changes to make but had a score to settle and then he was going to push his family out of the dope game because they had everything they needed already. He thought about Shay many nights after her death and although he loved Shonta dearly, his heart was somewhat attached to Shay the second she entered his life again. He never wanted for her to leave and chalked her up to be the one that got away. Now with her being dead, he knew all he had was Y.D. and he knew he'll die or go back to jail before he allowed anything happened to anyone of his kids, including Destiny. He had all kinds of thoughts going through his head- the studio, the love of his life, the new business and most of all, the plugs and connects. He been hearing how Shay got Luciano to give Lil' Rat them a better deal than he was paying and been coppin' from that Spanish mothafucka for years. Shay always had favoritism with Luciano and just thinking about how he got plugged in took him down memory lane.....

****

"Bae, your mama stay outta town," Fat Rat had snuck in Shay house from the back door because Shay mama Ronzie would always have her nosey neighbors keep an extra eye on the house while she was gone.

"I know, she with Luciano, some dude she met at the casino bout six months ago." Fat Rat sat in the living room sofa and noticed how in those six months Shay mama house became nicer and nicer.

"He must gotta check cause y'all starting to look like a middle wage family and if my memory is correct, your mother is on SSI." Shay busted out laughing and playfully punched Fat Rat.

"Don't worry 'bout my mama and for your info my mama got her a millionaire."

"Well, I want to marry you and meet him but if he leave your mama, I'm leaving you."

"Boy SHUT UP!" They were laughing and kickin it when the phone went off.

"Hello?....WHAT!...." Fat Rat knew something was wrong off the bat. He got up and walked to her and she fell into his arms crying.

"Mama been SHOT!" After grabbing the phone from her and speaking to a heavy Spanish accent male, he was told to take Shay to the airport and that the flights will be paid for if he'll see to it that she gets to the Bahamas safe. They later found out that Ronzie seen a strange man pull a gun in a crowd and aimed up toward Luciano while he wasn't looking and decided to risk her life for his. She passed a week later and with Fat Rat being there with her the whole way. He and Luciano became friends and he didn't turn back. He started seeing the most money he ever seen before and with money came bitches and then- Shay said she was pregnant. He didn't believe her *and* the money blinded him from paying attention to her. She felt so when she disappeared, he was like fuck her. Now as he sat in the garage with million dollars, he knew she made everything possible. He planned right then to visit her grave site and express himself once he took care of all the business. He got up and headed for the house and prepared to be the king he was before he left......

CHAPTER 10

"What time is it?" Shonta woke up and rolled over as she replayed last night. Snoop, who had been her boy toy the whole time Fat Rat was gone said, "It's 12:41." She jumped up "Shit!" She started rushing to get dressed and knew staying in a suite with Snoop the night before Fat Rat got out was a bad idea but with Snoop and his talk game about making the last night special, plus the liquor and cocaine he had her on allowed her thinking process to be off.

"Remember don't call me or come over cause he'll kill you. It was fun but it's over," she was talking and speeding tryna get herself together.

"What about me getting plugged in like you promised?"

"I told Boo I knew you from school, he agreed to front you a half a block, don't fuck up cause he'll kill you too. My family don't tolerate bullshit." Snoop got out the bed showing off his 247 pounds of pure muscle and height of 6'4 and walked up to Shonta and kissed her lightly.

"Let's go meatball," he said sarcastically and headed for the front door. By the time she made it home she could tell she fucked up by the note left in her side of the bed that read:

Meatball,

I came home, you wasn't there. I been to your shops, you wasn't there. I called you repeatedly, you didn't answer. The thrill of seeing you is leaving every second you gone and we starting off on the wrong foot. I've noticed the changes over the years, so I'm respecting your wish and going to find me a spot til you feel like sharing your life with me again. I know I did it to myself, so I accept responsibility.

Fat

The note wasn't what had her shaking. It was the picture of her and Snoop having dinner last night and the picture of them kissing told the whole story. All she could do was cry. She could only imagine how her life would change now that he knew.....

****

"Why you looking like that?" Samantha had just made it home from the shop and Boo was high as hell looking like he saw a ghost. He had just got the note from Mook Boy earlier and came home afterwards because he too understood the message far too well. Shay was like a mother to him too, growing up and he knew her just as well as her own son. Ten minutes before Samantha got home, Drama called Boo and told 'em that the lady in the picture in Young Dirty living room was the one seen coming outta the house. He and Ko-Ko had found out where Cat Daddy was and when they pulled up across the street, Shay was coming out so they say. It was fucking with Boo because Drama ain't know the lady on the picture was Shay and he was willing to bet his life in what he said with his own eyes. The note from Mook Boy made even more sense once he heard that from Drama, but he still ain't wanna be wrong or play with this brother which is why he was looking crazy but deep in thought.

"Do you believe in ghosts?" His facial expression didn't change but to Samantha, he got his point across. She just sat down next to him thinking about she phone call she got. Her lack of response gave him a feeling that Shay might've reach out to her also. He looked at her and said, "She ain't dead." It was more of a question then a statement.

"Please tell me we're talking 'bout the same person," she was shaking and now the verge of tears. "Please Bae!" She was crying now and all Boo could do is grab her and hold her while reality sunk in for both of them. It was bitter-sweet because they went through many nights of crying each other to sleep mourning off her death. Her being alive raised all kinds of questions and more importantly, do Young Dirty know and if not, who gone tell him.

"I ain't tell yo brother," Samantha said. Boo thought about what she said knowing everything they did after her death and the look in his road dawg eyes, he responded, "Me either." They both laughed lightly thinking how crazy Young Dirty was, then silence filled the living room again.

"Damn.... Why did she do it?" That was the question Boo asked himself and Samantha wanted to know but they both knew when the time comes, it'll be revealed. But until then, neither one of them would mention what they discovered.....

CHAPTER 11

The round table at the bulletproof had Fat Rat at the head of the table and Boo, Lil' Rat, Young Dirty, Mook Boy on both sides and the open seat where Shay used to be at the other end.

"First and foremost, all the extra stunning stops today unless you're a celebrity status like Mook Boy... Y.D., you put enough media work with the music to do some shinning, but your brother got his out tha mud. So why would you let him wear a million-dollar chain?" Fat Rat was speaking with authority and even though he asked a question, Young Dirty knew not to speak.

"Carlos and I had a talk today and he agreed to drop the ticket some more, so we pay fourteen a key for a thousand of them, but we must get a thousand and nothing less."

Boo said, "This will be a weekly thing so somebody needs to keep business moves on track and Lil' Rat, I'm putting you on it since you have so much free time."

Fat Rat continued, "Mook, I want to say I appreciate your loyalty and I'm glad to have you a part of this shit. Y.D., you need to pursue the music thing but that's just my opinion. I know Thug Mobb can be what you made it before. Mook, you got the hood happy and eating with D.B.M.G, you a real mothafuckin hustla' and no matter what, you a son of mine too. I am moving and when I get

44

my shit settled, everyone here will know where I'm located and no one else- and I mean no one." Lil' Rat had heard the situation and knew he was referring to Shonta. He disagreed with what his mother had done and he haven't spoke to her about it or even at all since finding out.

"I talked to Don Montiano lawyer and he got 'em a retrial and we need him here is that understood?" Everybody shook their heads knowing it was time to kidnap some family members of whoever will be in the jury box.

"We goin start taking family trips once a month from now on and we get experience with other countries before opening oversea accounts. Any questions?" Young Dirty then spoke up, "Trina pregnant just like Samantha." Lil' Rat looked over at his brother in disbelief. Everybody was quiet at the table. They had heard the rumors on tv too but knew how the media come up with anything.

"Be-Be too," Lil' Rat announced smiling at Young Dirty and Boo probably thought he was left out.

"We all gone be dads together nigga, don't count me out," Lil' Rat told 'em. They all talked about how crazy and fast shit going. Life is changing though for everybody and real fast.

"My life all gas, no brakes," Lil' Rat said. He explained how he first met Be-Be and at the end of the story, he told 'em who he found out her father was. That shocked the hell outta Fat Rat who's only comment was,

45

"It's a small world lil nigga, dat shit crazy." Mook Boy who was the only one without kids said, "Blood dem think it's easy Fat, but Lil' Rat club days finna stop and Boo and Dirt goin' to get tired of all the random requests from they baby mamas. Shit, I hope that pregnant shit ain't contagious." They laughed and kicked shit a lil while longer till the realtor called Fat Rat phone letting him know she was on her way to his future new home...

****

"Uncle Dugo..." Carlos embraced his only Uncle and took a seat in his office.

"Carlos, I'm not going to play around with the concern. It was brought to my attention of your shipments being took either by the police or pirates. It don't fucking matter you're costing the family money. I lost $18 million in this last shipment and you're gambling millions at a time with something that's supposed to be proof-detected, meaning undetectable...... If I lose another penny in any other shipment, you will become food." Carlos listened and kept his poker face. He was 38 hot inside. He ain't know how to tell his Uncle that he lost over half the shipment money gambling, which is why he had to say the police got it. He had never been addicted to anything but the fact that he couldn't win made him keep trying because he felt determined to do so and ended up in too deep.

"Money runs this family hunh? Money and NOT family!" He screamed at his Uncle whose composure never change as he listened to what his favorite nephew had to say.

"If it's money that make us family, then money is the focus for now on. Will that make you happy? Will dat make you NOT put me on da plate?!" As Dugo listened he knew his nephew was right. He just wanted to get his point across because family had started losing and the family never lose.

"You do your best to see to it that your business is handled correctly and there will be no plate. Now, who is the family first you spoke of," his Uncle changed the subject as if the last conversation was over. Carlos took some time before speaking allowing himself to calm down. He really ain't want to speak on the black kids buying twice as much as his biggest customer.

"The father of the family called and we made very good progress. He sent a hundred grand for his appreciation which I gave Auntie Linda, but his business is strictly through part of every shipment." He wanted his Uncle to know that he was more than capable to serve the black family.

"I would like to meet the father one day soon. Get his first and last name. See what he was locked up for. I hope he don't be a bruise to this family in her long run because bruises are not good." Carlos had heard enough.

47

He stood and said, "NO Dents, NO Bruises, No Food," then walked out.

CHAPTER 12

"Luciano did this, Luciano did that, you know what my friend? You have no balls. And you surely don't know nothin' bout me or my family." The officer that was tied and gaged didn't care about anything that was said. All they wanted was his life. He knew he was playing a dangerous game following the black female that had been around the family lately. Now here he was in an unknown warehouse with Mr. Luciano himself.

"What is it you were looking for. A confession? You wanted someone to say Mr. Officer, I traffic cocaine and kill people huh?!" The officer who had his head down the whole time praying looked up and that was all it took to send Luciano in rage.

"POP!! "AHHH!" the officer screamed through the gag in pain from the .357 shot to the knee.

"You like Pain Pig?!" POP!! He shot the other knee, "Now you listen real good-" Before he could finish they both heard heels walking towards them. Shay walked directly behind the officer and gave him a shot to the dome.

"POP!!!... Fuck playing Papi, we kill and keep it movin'. I'm hungry, let's go eat." Luciano just smiled and held out his arm for her to join him and they left the officer there to be found whenever. Once in the Porsche Spyder, Luciano looked over and said, "He told me where your snitch is staying, so tomorrow we get your life back." Shay just laid back her seat and closed her eyes.

"I'll be glad when I can hug my kids again." There was nothing Luciano could say so he just pulled off determined to be there for Shay like her mother was there for him and he was willing to put his life on the line also the same way....

****

"Ko-Ko unlocked the back door, we pulling up." Ko-Ko hung up the phone and headed to the back of the trap. He and Drama had Tremain Street bumpin'. George watched the front of the trap including the roads and waved Drama into the backyard with the .45 ready for any jack boy that might've peeped the move. Once the moving truck was unloaded and the trap was secured, all of them started calling they people to let them know it's a green light. PeeWee Longway's, "Do it for my young niggaz," played in the entertainment set while the big screen showed all the cameras.

"What we working with," George said coming back in and locking the burglar bars behind him.

"200 pounds of pressure and 60 squares of dat clean shit," Drama said while testing the pressure out.

"Ko-Ko, how much money you got on you big home?" Ko-Ko pulled some blue hunnits out his pocket and started counting. He wanted to do it too.

"I got 'bout $3,100- Let shoot," George pulled out his money and said, "I got 'bout $1,100- Let me win some of y'all money," the dice game started from there. By night-time Boo, Lil' Rat, Red Clid, Young Dirty, Fat Rat, Spook, and 'bout three more niggas from da hood was going at it.

"Lil Joe let's go," Lil' Rat said as he shook the dice. It was at least eight grand on the ground cause they moved the dice game outside.

"Show dat 25 wit' no bullets," Spook told 'em looking for a 2 and a 5 to show so he could pick-up. They were all having fun smoking and drinking like the normal days in Slumpville goes when Cat pulled up.

"Jitt, come fuck with me." Cat was Gally Gal road dawg everybody knew her from fucking with Dip which was Spook brother. Young Dirty walked over to where she was sitting outside her car.

"What's good sis," he said because most of Slumpville considered themselves family.

"I need some money to go see bae this weekend and he wanted me to ask you to send him some weed too."

"Say no mo," Young Dirty pulled out $500 and gave it to her then told her to hold up and walked back to the dice game.

"Say George go grab a bag of gas and everybody give me a hunnit dollars for Dip." No one complained, they all did it with no questions. Even tho Spook ain't been out long, he gave three hunnit to 'em and they all stated back gambling. After George came back with the gas and his hunnit, Young Dirty walked back to Cat.

"Here sis this for him and you too toward the bills and yo lil girl." Cat hugged Young Dirty and said, "Preciate it and Gal said she need to see you when you leave here because she know something you should know."

"Check... Tell her I'll be over there in 'bout an hour."

"Alright....Thank y'all," Cat screamed out at the dice game.

"It's all luv sis. I'ma get it back from these niggas anyway. Ain't that right Lil' Rat," said Spook. Lil' Rat hit his point right after that and said, "Hell Nah, sis this nigga might be calling you to borrow some money so don't go far!" Everybody laughed including Spook, and Cat left with a smile. When the game was over only Drama and Fat Rat had lost but neither was upset. Money was coming so good for everybody that wanted grade A dope or pressure, they had to hit Slumpville. People started calling Lake County, Cake County cause all the money that came to that mothafucka. Ko-Ko played some instrumentals in the entertainment set and everybody took turns rappin' even when they didn't know how. Weed gave people that courage. Before they knew it, it was about 12:30 at night and everybody was still out there.

"Trina still calling, plus I'm still feeling good, should I go lay the wood or stay posted in the hood," Y.D. was slidin' da beat and everybody was rockin' wit'em.

"When mama lost her life, I was left with a plan, popz was in da feds and I was forced to be a man. Me and brah turnt 40 to 100 grand, now we hood millionaires. We wasn't mothafuckas playin'!" His phone rung and he finally stopped rappin' and said he had to go. Everybody gave him his pro's and he could tell his daddy wanted to start back rappin' for real by his comments, but he had already made a vow to himself. He went home and fucked Trina all night and morning because did some reason, his spirit was still lifted from yesterday. Gally Gal had called and text, but he never noticed because he always was doing something else at the time and he had really forgot. If he would've knew that Shay was there waiting on him, he would've probably been there but being in the blind, he missed a time he dreamed of almost every night......

CHAPTER 13

"Bitch, you think it's a game- Set fire to this Pimp C wannabe." After giving the orders from Kyrie, Re-Re, which was the worse of the Hustleville hit squad of girls, cut the torch on and placed it directly in front of Butterball, a Tampa brick boy face. She fried his cries for help, then they tore up the spot looking for the stash. Kyrie, Re-Re, Ke-Ke, and Tweet had been playing and laying on niggas since freshman year in high school when Tweet got raped. Their crew elevated quick to murder for hire and hits like this one that they were caring out.

"Got It!" Tweet said with her Haitian accent as if she just came to the U.S yesterday. There before her eyes, was not only the six hundred, fifty grand that was said to be there that they can keep, but the black book with all the info on all big-time bettas and big speeding gamblers. They had to bring back for the other half of the $2 million dollars for getting the book and bringing it back. They left 13th street in Tampa with thirteen bricks of boy, thirty-three bricks of girl and black book, plus another seven bodies under their belts but "*Who's counting*" was their motto. On the way home from the move they just pulled, Ke-Ke said to the group of three, "This book gotta be worth more than they paying for it if they willing to dish out $2 mill for this mothafucka." Re-Re responded to her sister, "Child-Boo, fuck that book. I know they betta have the rest of our bread cause I ain't killin' fo' free bitch!" The ghetto sistas high fived each other and Kyrie who was in deep thought, asked all the girls a question.

"Do y'all remember them D.B.M.G niggas at the festival we were looking at? Dem young niggas da rapper Young Dirty be talking bout in songs?"

"Yeh me remember, that bum! The one they call Drama is the one that didn't know how to keep his hands to himself."

Tweet added, "Bitch please, you know you was all in that nigga grill. We all know dats your taste trick." They all laughed at Re-Re comment. Kyrie cut the music that was playing in the the background completely off and said while driving, "I think we can hit 'em." This got all the girls attention. They were used to hitting big boy licks and clearing rich folks kinda paper, but they also knew a lotta big dawgs rarely put in work, so they were more pussy then there soldiers- but every mothafucka in D.B.M.G and First Family lived the life they spoke of.

"You talking about Drama them, or tha First Family cause you know Fat Rat done got out," Ke-Ke mentioned.

"Bitch you scared? Let's hit 'em," Re-Re said getting wound up. "We goin do it but we goin' do it right. When we do tho, it's gone be our last one because these niggas is strapped, so let's all try to remember everything about these niggas. It's time to hit our last lick.".....

****

Shonta was sitting at home eating Mc Donald's, thinking 'bout Fat Rat. She had been doing both for weeks now, really since she had read the letter from him the day he was released. Her son took Fat Rat side on the situation and she ain't blame 'em, she fucked up. Today she decided would be the last day she'd mourn or wait on him to come back through the door because a woman she had pride also. Snoop had been texting even after she told him not to, so she guessed he heard 'bout her and Fat Rat splitting up. She thought on how Snoop didn't lack much from being what Fat Rat was and she knew if she had to be with Snoop, that she'll still be straight, but her gut and heart just wouldn't allow her to not be able to be a real family. She always thought the motto was *"Family First."* This brought more tears to her eyes and got her upset too. How could Fat Rat just leave her for cheating? He ain't no angel. So what, he fucked bitches left and right and she didn't leave his fat ass. Fuck him if he think I'ma be round this bitch crying in shit. She got up from the sofa and went to the phone. She had some shit on her mind that she wanted to let him know.

"The number you dialed has been changed or disconnected-" she hung up and screamed. How dare he change his number and not give it to her? If this the way he wanna play, then that's how we'll do it. She grabbed her

56

keys and got Destiny dressed and headed out the door. Her next move might be deadly but it was a war that Fat Rat started...

CHAPTER 14

"It's so much I want to say, but it's too late now lil mama ... Just know a nigga never stopped loving you," Fat Rat was at Shay grave site letting it all out. "Me and Shonta no longer together, which you already know. It's fucked up how on the night before I got out, she was fucking so good she couldn't even be there to get me from the gate. I know if you was here, you would've been there regardless." It was late in the evening so it was getting dark which is why Fat Rat didn't see Shay behind him the whole time. She heard it all.

"I thought about you as much or maybe even more than her when I was gone. Crazy ain't it?" He laughed lightly to himself and continued. "The night when I called before you left the hood and headed to Apopka and it said your number didn't work no mo, I admit I told myself you was just trippin'. Hell, I didn't even think you was pregnant for real. Our life could've been so different if you would've stayed lil mama." By now he was breaking down right in front of her which was something she never saw and it had her with tears in her eyes also. She couldn't take any more of it and disappeared unnoticed and went back in the vehicle she had rented under a fake name. She was crying like a baby. She had been holding so much in tryna be strong for her son, that she locked all her memories she had with Fat Rat out of her heart. He spoke about her mother's incident and all while she was behind him and now all the old feeling she had for him came back and she listened to him confess. After crying for so long, she looked up and he was gone. She told herself next time she'll be the one confessing and whatever happens, happens. With that thought she crunk up her car and pulled off.....

****

"Who dat bitch that was with 'em?" Re-Re and Tweet was doing the research and watching Fat Rat every move. They didn't know the broad that walked up behind him then walked off minutes later, but they did know that he was at Shay grave which was Young Dirty mother. They all had heard stories 'bout her and how gangsta she was when she was alive and they all wanted to have that same legendary memory when they die. They seen Fat Rat head to his 600 Benz and focused back on him to Sanford, which was Seminole County but Central Florida, and leave out a restaurant with two duffle bags that he did not go in with. Now they was hoping he was headed to the stash house since it was getting dark, that way they'll know where everything's at. They slowly pulled out in traffic three cars behind him laying on their ticket out of the game for good......

****

"Bitch you lying," Trina said shocked at the news of Butterball which was a nigga she used to fuck with death. After hearing how he died, she said a prayer for him to God. Butterball treated her right and if it wasn't for her now baby daddy fucking her head up and locking her in, she would've probably still be with him and doing funeral arrangements right now. She finished her conversation with her ghetto ass cousin and did a walk through their new place which she picked out. Young Dirty told her it was a baby present which she have been getting a lot of lately. Her baby was happy to be having a baby and she only could smile because she was happy to be having one too especially by the one she chose to have one with. He completed her and when she was around him, she felt accepted and loved as herself and not Trina, Da Baddest Bitch. She had made it all the way upstairs and through it and headed downstairs when she spotted her. There sitting on the sofa crying silently was her man mama alive in the flesh and it scared the hell outta her.

"I don't know what type of shit you're on, but my man mama been dead," she cocked her Trina trophy that had thirty in the clip. "You can speak now or let me figure it out on my own at your funeral." She couldn't believe somebody had the balls to act like his mama and the only thing she was thinking was that it was a robbery and she wasn't going out like Willy Lump Lump, she was going out Remy Ma style. Shay didn't even look up when she said,

"Shit finna change for us, but us ladies are going to have to stick together. It won't last forever but they going take my son. Mook, Boo, and Lil' Rat too. We gone get 'em back. I went away to make sure of that. You could tell him I'm still alive and everything I'm telling you, and that they're all goin' be took, but I prefer you help me make sure they come home quick as possible." By now Trina had lowered her weapon and was all ears. From what she was hearing it sounded like the feds was headed their way and Shay had a plan to make sure they beat the charges.

"I'm in," Trina said without thinking twice, ready to do whatever for her nigga that she refused to go without....

CHAPTER 15

"This is the best view of downtown Orlando if I must say. It's a best buy," the white lady realtor had just finished showing Fat Rat around the five-bedroom, three-bathroom baby mansion with a three-car garage and ocean view that came with being at the top of the hill the community was built on. The look she had been giving him let him know she knew he was a dope boy, but also screamed she liked it.

"You can pay the whole $250 thousand in one payment or put a down payment of $25 thousand and move in tomorrow," her professional speech didn't do nothing to hide her interest.

"I'll get with my lawyer and he'll handle the funds but just so you know, there will only be one payment," he knew with her hearing that and how much commission she'll pocket, she would be excited.

"Well, I guess that sums up our business, but if you need me for anything and I mean anything," she said while walking up to Fat Rat as he just stood there looking back into her eyes letting her know he was ready when she was.

"...Don't hesitate to call." She then handed him her business card with her number on the back then walked and got in her Lexus. Fat Rat had to take a second to breathe after she was gone because she left his dick rock hard but he knew now wasn't the time or the place. He headed to his car and while putting his key to the door he seen a reflection of the female behind him bouncing off the driver window, but the female saw behind him was supposed to be dead. He turned around and was face to face with Shay herself looking better than he remembered.

"Let me drive, we need to talk..."

****

"This bitch swole all the time ain't it," Boosie and Webbie was at the park on Highland Ave with Boo and Mook Boy, blowing mango after a three-song session at Fat Rat studio.

"Main, dat bitch thea hoarse thick," Webbie said talking 'bout Jack-Jack which was Gally Gal sister. "I'm fucking fo I leave, I swear fo God!" Boosie replied. As usual it was a car show in the parking lot and a block party in da park by now everybody came out to pay respect for Boo who was throwing a "Write yo Dawg Day" party. There was two picture booths and Boo supplied all the stamps, pens, notepads, and envelopes. Boosie and Webbie was taking pictures with folks that were writing somebody locked up. Samantha was under the pavilion with a laptop looking up anybody name that someone didn't know the address to. When Kesha walked passed, Webbie his mind was made up. She was too Florida to him for him not to want to have her. From her dreads to her mouth full of golds and chocolate complexion, the fact she waked by blowing the same kind of reefa they was smoking was enough to show her boss status and he ain't hide the fact he was hooked.

"I'ma holla at y'all in a bit ya heard me," with that said he was gone and went over to the picnic table where her and her homegirls from Hustleville were giggling and smoking. 'Bout ten minutes later her and Webbie was leaving the park and Boo and Boosie just made eye contact cause both knew what was finna happen. Mook Boy was high as hell tryna explain to Blackberry that he didn't mean any disrespect when he in boxed her on Facebook saying, "Fuck sumthin'." It wasn't long till he too was leaving with her. Samantha, Boo, and Boosie was all kickin shit when Be-Be and Lil' Rat showed up. Something was different about Be-Be and Samantha called it out ASAP.

"Bitch you Pregnant!" she said out loud excitedly. Be-BE busted out laughing and the girls embraced each other both over excited.

"It's true lil bruh?" Boo asked Lil' Rat while smiling because he already knew. "Yeah you pregnant too," he said messing with Samantha. Samantha's phone ranged and she picked up the second ring.

"Meet me at Publix, don't bring nobody or tell nobody," and just like that the phone call ended leaving Samantha's heart racing. Shay had just reached out and she wasn't yet prepared for their reunion. She still kinda didn't believe she was alive but that question was answered now so she told Boo that she was headed to Publix to get some more meat in hopes of getting all the other answers she need....

****

"ALL RISE!" everybody in the courtroom stood up including Don Montiano and his half a million-dollar lawyer. The head of the jury had his life in his hands on a white piece of paper and after the judge said for everyone to be seated, Montiano focused in on all of their faces. He will later identify them and have 'em all killed if they found him guilty and take his life. The last eleven months in the County wasn't the worse due to him being who he was and him having over $20k on his books. Hearing Fat Rat had got released made him wish he was there on the outside with 'em. Fat Rat couldn't visit him because in order to visit you had to at least been out a year. When he looked back though, Fat Rat was in the stands with Lil' Rat, Boo, Young Dirty and Tasha who had been there every visitation and court date holding him down.

"Your Honor, the jury have reached a verdict," the short older Spanish woman stated. "We the people of the court find Lamontez Hinton not guilty on all charges." The courtroom erupted with chatter. For Spaulding County to lose a trial was rare and Fox 5 was there reporting the shocking verdict. The judge hit his gravel repeatedly

"ORDER HERE! ORDER IN HERE! Are you sure that's the decision all of you agreed to?" The jury leader stood again.

"Yes, your Honor, the jury feels there wasn't enough evidence to convict Mr. Evans." The courtroom erupted in chatter again. Don Montiano leaned back in his chair with a smile on his face and the media was eating it up. It wasn't until he looked at Fat Rat and the look on *his* face that made him straighten up and drop the smile. He remembered everything Fat Rat taught 'em and knew that no media is good media. He had been fucking with his hood rat and got tricked back to Georgia and after a fye fuck session at the "W," the bitch called the folks on 'em tryna collect $10k award, which lead them to the studio to arrest him and in the end, costed her life. Lil' Rat and everybody else proved to be there for him and his Mobb brothers didn't miss a beat going as far as dropping the pack off so he could flood the county and smoke good too. One letter he got from Lil' Rat decoded them being young millionaires and he had plans on expanding up back home since the case wasn't over his head. He already was ending shit to his brothers for a good ticket, but he knew with him being back, he was finna go ham but for right now, he just wanted to leave.

"Can we go?" He leaned over and asked his lawyer. The judge, announcing he was a free man, answered his question so he stood up and Tasha ran into his arms with a face full of tears.

"Real gangstas don't die baby girl, I told you the law can't kill me," was all he said as he hugged her and walked out of the courtroom and made arrangements to get his property that was still at the county.....

CHAPTER 16

"You swear this shit goin work?" Samantha was talking to Shay while they both walked up to the unknown address in material that a couple of Jehovah Witnesses would wear with books and bibles in their hands.

"Have I ever let you down?" she responded as they made it to the door. Slick had told Lil' Rat that he was going to Detroit where his family was and would be back in a month but never returned. Lil' Rat took it as if he decided to stay and would reach out to him once he was established. He even had a million put up for whenever he did reach back out to him due to the fact both of Slick's phones was off a week after he left. Slick tried to get some niggas to kid nap Shay in hopes of hitting the jackpot, but Luciano had found out about Slick cooperating with the feds and caught up with his crew after having someone watch him and shot it out, then faked Shay death to buy them some time to handle the situation before the feds stepped in. Hearing Shay was killed is what scared Slick of knowing he would die once the truth was revealed and he was glad his cousin was the REAL person who sent the hit squad and not him because his cousin is dead now and he still alive. His cousin was from Detroit but told folks he was from Atlanta to throw off anyone that questioned so slick wasn't linked to it. Luciano knew though and now it was time to pay Slick a visit.

"POP!POP!POP! ... POP!..." Both Samantha and Shay looked at each other crazy as hell as gunfire went off in the house. Before they knew what happened, Slick was shooting out the front door going a hunnit miles an hour and knocking them down in the process. When Samantha and Shay started to get up and looked, Boo had met Slick from the opposite direction and had a Sawed off 12-gage pointed directly at his skull.

"Make me do it Pussy! Move so I could cancel yo' snitching ass out here in da middle of the road," Slick was beyond scared. He put his hands up to surrender but Boo felt tried cause he told 'em not to move and he did it.

"BOMB!!!" Slick whole head exploded all over the streets. Sirens could be heard and Lil' Rat and Drama came from out the house with gloves on and Lil' Rat ran straight to Shay and hugged her.

"Don't ever do us like that again," she said while expressing his real love for Shay the saying, "Let's get the FU- I mean heck out of here." He smiled at the old feeling of having not to curse around both his mama, it was a good feeling too. Once everyone was safely away from the scene, Lil' Rat explained that they followed her and out two and two together. "Ma, brah still don't know cause we feel that's something you'll have to tell 'em." Shay understood completely and didn't want anyone to tell him but her, which is why she did what she did how she did it.

"I would of been told his young hot ass if he wasn't so far up Trina's." They all laughed knowing how fucked up he was about Trina who was the getaway driver. "I'm going over there tonight so y'all be ready to celebrate when I'm done talking to 'em... Shit I'm back," and with that said she was back, the queen of the squad...

CHAPTER 17

Billy Ray just called, so I know dat play at least 200,

Hood millionaire still grindin' getting trap money.

A million waves, a thousand tats, Bitch,

I'm young Dirty D, Da Baddest Bitch my baby mama,

so we stay on T.M.Z.

The value done went down, cause I fogged out da coupe,

Extendo on da fin, headed to drop off a deuce

He want a brick, but I don't know 'em,

Shit'd, so diz what we goin do.

Get his money, meet me at da park, n I'ma serve you.

Young Dirty had dropped his first song in the studio in a long time and was riding down Highland Ave listening to what might be the single of the album. He had the top down on his 72 Donk and the six twelves beating while his thirty-inch billionaires floated as he glided through the hood. He pulled in Jump yard, which was a nigga from the hood he grew up reppin' Highland Ave and Jackson Street with because they both got money at that four way when they was headfirst. Jump had an Uncle that smoked crack and wash cars in Jump yard to stay high and Young Dirty was feeling good and decided to get his candy bowling ball green and chrome dope mobile washed while he kicked shit in his land. He felt his hood was a jungle, but he was the Zookeeper. He had killas on call and money for anybody from his hood that went to jail. It was times like this that made hustlin' all worth it. He was blowing Mook Boy favorite, which was mango kush while listening to his track again when his mother popped in his head. He had so much shit built up inside of him that he just started flowing off the beat that was playing. Jump grabbed his iPhone and started recording and Young Dirty didn't even notice as he spoke on what was going through his head-

Mama left for dead, now the niggas killed her dead too.
Baby on the way,
I hate to say it but I don't know what to do.
Everybody strait and thank you GOD they ain't kill Mook
D.B.M.G Bitch! if you ain't that then nigga fuck you!

He was in his own world and Jump was getting it all on camera and feeling his words at the same time. He went for almost ten minutes cause the track was on repeat. Not once did he fuck up while spitting and you could tell that none of it was written. Jump uploaded it to his Facebook and the views went crazy. Young Dirty paid Jumps Uncle hopped in his ride and headed to 441. He needed to just ride and clear his mind. Sometimes he felt that nobody could understand the shit he been through in life. Within 40 minutes, he found himself deep in Orlando on E. He pulled into the first gas station he seen and jumped out to get some gas and blunts and left the car running. First thing he noticed was a van park in front of the gas station with four niggas dressed in all black. They were all staring at him coming from his ride and looked as if they just stopped the conversation when he pulled up. It also looked like they had something else on their mind. With Young Dirty mind so clouded, he was hoping they gave him a reason to unload the extendo he had and unload some pressure at the same time. When he made it to where they were, he mugged all of 'em just to give off a bad vibe then entered the store ...

Snoop and his cousins were at the local gas station in his hood plotting on their next move. His nose habit and bad decisions was how he blowed through the brick he paid for along with the two bricks he had fronted to him by Boo. Between that, losing the dice game, and tricking off playing the King of the World .. Actually he didn't even really know how he blowed the bricks and money he had because shit in his life had been moving so fast lately. What he did know was that he needed to get some bread up quick or he would be going to war real soon. His cousin that owed him a favor was doing big shit in Atlanta with his squad of killas, and he knew that him and the rest of the G.F. members would ride for the cause if his cousin tell 'em, but he might not need 'em because it a quick come up had just pulled in to get gas and didn't even know that he wouldn't leave the way he come.

"Man you seen that fuck nigga muggin?" one of his cousins asked him already riled up. He too noticed the violent look the familiar face gave the group and him looking familiar was the only thing that kept Snoop from giving the green light right then.

"Say do any of y'all know that nigga?" After Snoop asked that question, the wildest cousin out the bunch spoke up.

"Fuck who that is, he left dat bitch crunk so it's mines now." He started heading towards the vehicles and halfway there, the gas station door opened and bullets went off...

****

"Yeah, I know it's a least $3 million in the house and ain't no telling how many bricks and pounds are there," Shonta had went against the grain and was now setting up Fat Rat to get robbed. She found out where Fat Rat stayed by following him and now had three flunkies ready to get rich and she was ready for revenge. The last time she seen Fat Rat, he was with another bitch and it broke her heart and turned her cold. She thought they were going to be able to talk it out seeing how she forgave him for all his cheating.

"Tonight is the night, all or nothing," she told the three young niggas that was listening to her every word and doing math. She smiled on the inside knowing the Fat

Rat wouldn't even know what hit 'em, but it damn sho was going to be what he deserved.

CHAPTER 18

Tweet and the rest of the girls were parked two blocks away from Fat Rat spot. They had seen enough duffle bags go inside his house to know it was in there. They had came up with a foolproof plan to get in and out swiftly. They all tightened up there silencers and prepared for their last big lick.

"This is it ladies, no fuck ups but no second guessing. If something seems wrong, we shoot first and ask questions later. Y'all ready?" Re-Re responded to Kyrie by saying, "I just want this shot to be over so I can go to a beach somewhere and kick my feet up."

"Bitch, you gone do more than kick your feet up," Tweet said and the girls shared a light laugh and exited the vehicle. Kyrie and Ke-Ke jumped in the taxi that was two houses down waiting on them.

"Where to?" the driver asked.

"We're tourist and we got lost on our walk but looking for 426 Hilton Drive." The cab driver knew the street was two blocks over but decided to make it a 30-minute ride anyway which the girls knew he would do with them being tourists. Their plan was officially in effect....

****

"Man how tha fuck you get too drunk to drive, you a fool," Fat Rat was headed out the house while on the phone with Peanut who was drunk as a skunk and backed in on Grantside, seeing shit in 3D.

"I'm on my way and you betta have some C.F. and some gas money Big Boy," they both laughed and Fat Rat ended the call. Once outside he pushed the button on his key chain that opened his garage and decided to go with something fast. He jumped in his Bentley GT Continental Couple with the turbo boost. He was far from dumb and knew when something wasn't right, so when the two females in that walked by his driveway on his way pulling out was so out of place in this residential area full of rich with folks he lived at.

"Oh niggaz think shit sweet," he said to himself while driving and looking in his rearview mirror. He grabbed his phone at a stop sign while calling Lil' Rat. Before Lil' Rat could pick up, a van came to a stop across from his with a young black dude driving and confirmed his assumptions. He knew what time it was and if the young dude driving would have did his homework, he would have known that the Bentley at the stop sign with him (with the five percent tints) was his target and the car was purchased two days ago, but that lack of info made the young dude the target instead. Fat Rat pulled away from the stop sign and kept straight, instead of making the left he was supposed to because he wanted to see exactly how many was in the van.

77

He knew by getting a close look at driver, whoever it was, couldn't be a threat. Who have kids do a man's job? He also knew the alarm system at his house would have the police there within three minutes if a mothafucka was to try to break-in, which he was fine with since he gave the situation some thought and decided that he just won't come back home tonight and he'll deal with the situation tomorrow if it's still a situation to deal with. Nothing was in the house beside close to $400k which no one would ever find, not even the police so he wasn't worried about taking a loss. $400k wasn't shit these days. But he still wanted to know who wanted him bad enough to come to where he lay his head. Since he been released the only enemy he made was his baby mama and as far as he knew, she ain't know where he rested at. Lil' Rat phone had went to voicemail for the second time so he just cut up the Mook Boy he had bumpin' and headed to the Lake while thinking who could be at him......

****

"Shay girl, you on some bullshit for making a bitch think you dead hoe. I spent rent money on that dress I wore to your funeral." Seeing her friend alive and healing brought happiness to Gally Gal, but she being who she was had to talk some shit too.

"I see you doing damn good tho like the rest of the family, let me find out you was somewhere having fun while I was crying over yo black ass," she said with fake anger while smiling.

"Bitch you know I had to come from the dead to see yo crazy ass!" They laughed and continued to talk shit and drink on Grantside where Red Clid had it pumpin' at. Peanut was across the street asleep in the car and they laughed and joked about that too. Shay felt good being back around everybody that she considered family. She still kept a low profile so if you wasn't out there then you might not knew she was alive. A text came to her phone saying to check her Facebook, which she did and seen her son expressing himself and she seen the pain in his eyes. It brought tears to hers because when she went to tell him she was alive she froze up and turned around. Now she felt guilty because everyone knew but him.

"Girl what's wrong?" Gal asked, concerned when she seen Shay start to cry.

"I gotta go find my son," was all Shay said before heading to her rental she still had. Boo had just seen the video with his brother rapping and wanted to tell him what he thought he already knew. He was a little upset at Shay for not letting him know already that she wasn't dead. He tried Young Dirty phone twice and twice it went to voicemail. He was home with Samantha spending quality time but knew his brother needed him at the moment which is why he was headed out the door to find him. Something told him to grab his Ruger so he did and went to locate his other half because anybody that seen the video knew he had murder on his mind. And Boo really knew because he seen that look in Young Dirty eyes way to many times growing up hitting licks. Samantha was crampin' so she didn't put up a fight about Boo leaving. She just locked the house up behind him after getting her hug and kiss and headed to her room. She knew Young Dirty was upset because she too watched the video with Boo, and she also knew the only person that can talk to him was Boo. She only prayed he found him in time and that they both was safe.....

CHAPTER 19

"That'll be $64.95," the female at the register told Young Dirty before recognizing who he really was.

"Oh shit! It's You!" She was surprised and excited to be in the presence of the celebrity that put Central Florida on the map. Young Dirty mind was still on the niggas outside when he passed her a hunnit dollar bill, grabbed his swishas and headed for the door. On his way out he seen one of the dudes that was at the van headed to his Vert and that was all he needed to see. He drew his extendo and came out the door bussin'.

"BOOM! BOOM! BOOM!" All three slugs hit his target and caught everybody at the van off guard which left them sitting ducks.

"BOOM! BOOM! BOOM! BOOM!" Four bullets dropped two of the three that was left as one of them that looked like the head of the pack ran round the van taking cover. Young Dirty was zoned out, he wasn't worried 'bout the pussy that ran and finished both off with head shots.

"BOOM! BOOM!" Then went to the other one that was heading to his ride when he was in the store and finished him too.

"BOOM! BOOM! BOOM!" He then jogged back in the store where the female at the register that witnessed the whole thing was. She was gone. He searched throughout the store but she was nowhere. He ran back out to the store and began pumping gas knowing he didn't have long before the police showed up. He knew he had fucked up but what could he do now. Once was he heard the first sound of sirens, he took the nozzle out and jumped in his Donk then fled....

****

"Mr. Griffin, I'll have a car ready for you. Is that all you need?" Michael looked in the evidence bag at the video tapes of the murder committed on Puncho by Shay. He lied and said he needed to review them to go towards the case he's building in the First Family. The truth was, Lil' Rat had his baby girl gagged and naked ducked taped somewhere unknown and she was only 4 years old, so if whoever wanted the tapes would go to that extreme, then he could only imagine what they would do if he didn't comply.

"Yes, that'll be all Shirley," he replied before walking out and switching bags with the female on the curb right before his ride pulled up. He was told if he did things successfully, then his little angel will be at his home and that's exactly where he was headed.

"It's official," Trina said to Shay on the phone after seeing the tapes were there in the bag once she had made it around the corner and into her car. Shay opened the driver door to her car and let the little girl out the backseat and kneeled down to have a few last words.

82

"Now go across the street and wait for your father, okay?" When the little girl heard that her father was coming, she became excited. She enjoyed eating happy meals and playing games at the place the lady speaking to her told her was daycare, but she was ready to go home. She zeroed in one here she was to wait and realized she was home.

"Thank you Miss Lady for watching me," she said sincerely. Shay smiled at her good manners and walked her to the porch. Once back in the car she texted Michael to hurry home, then turned the power off on the phone. She would later throw it out the window and forgot the whole situation. She just needed to handle the situation before the feds came, which she knew was coming. She had been calling her son phone for three days now and had been staying at his house but he never answered or came home. She found herself praying again for what seemed like the fiftieth time that everything was okay. Fat Rat had told her about almost being robbed or killed by a unknow assassin and with dealing with trying to get to the bottom of that, and dealing with clearing the family name, plus trying to find her son, she was stressed and needed and wanted a massage. While thinking that she decided to go to the new massage spot that recently was built in Sorrento, five minutes outside if the hood. She arrived in forty because where she came from was that far. She seen Shonta white Porsche soon as she pulled in. The fact that Shonta might ain't know she was alive, made Shay think twice about going in. She had too much going on to have to go through still being alive- Fat Rat leaving her and all that other shit. On second thought, she remembered Fat Rat saying Shonta was a suspect in his situation, so it might be good to wait and follow her to see where she go....

****

By myself in the room, high as hell countin'...
100, 200, 300, 400 thousand
I heard that 12 looking for me so I'm on the run,
And if I get caught with all this, I won't have no bond.

Young Dirty was couped up in the Marriott preparing to make an exit for good, due to him knowing he had fucked up. He was writing his last song describing his present predicament. He was ready to leave Florida for good and wanted to take Trina with him. No one knew where he was and he didn't answer no calls and only read texts, most asking where he was at. Although he knew fucked up by murdering niggas in public like he did, for some reason he didn't care. His mother was killed in the middle of the hood for everyone to see, so that made all the safe shit go out the window in his mind. Trina on the other hand was another story. He knew she was worried like crazy bout him and he felt bad taking her and his unborn thru something like this even though he didn't think like that when the shit happened. He wanted to call her and let her know so they could flee the country together but didn't want to put the burden on her for his actions. He had been watching the news from what the reporters said, they didn't have any leads. He knew the store had cameras because he seen the screens behind the counters himself. He figured they wanted to get him first and the best way to get him would be him going home or calling Trina so he didn't do either. Now he was smoking and drinking himself crazy, trying to plan his next move. One thing he know fa sho, was that he would be in Canada by next weekend....

CHAPTER 20

"Why the fuck isn't it here yet!?!" Carlos was mad as fuck while waiting on his shipment. The only good news was that the black girls he paid had proven to pull through and had the black book that would give him the advantage he needed to see extra money and when he say money, he meant *millions*. They were scheduled to deliver it tonight at one of his restaurants so he was running behind schedule. He seen the cargo ship headed to the dock and smiled. He loved when a hood plan came together. Not three minutes after, the cargo ship stopped, did Coast Guards come from everywhere. He was left shocked and felt he jinxed himself for lying last time. It wasn't until they started going in the ship did he leave knowing they came for his dope. He thought about his Uncle's comment and knew he had fucked up. How he needed the black book and then some to get outta this.

"FUCK!!!" He screamed to himself as he hit the steering wheel. As he was pulling off his phone ranged. He looked down and seen it was Boo, the black rich kid. An idea formed in his head which would most likely kill their relationship but fix his with his Uncle. He weighed his options.

"Fuck dem mooley's," he said to himself and pulled off after a light chuckle.....

"Bitch, how the fuck you didn't see shit?" Kyrie was furious. They had planned everything to the tee and came out empty.

"Who the fuck was in da van?" She asked next while speeding trying to figure out their next move. They had been laying low because they had to shoot their way out of robbery that would've left them straight for life. When the taxi brought them to the address, a van was pulling out. Tweet came from around the house shooting like she lived there. Kyrie gave the taxi a shot to the head and sealed his fate while to her blind, the 4th of July came early. Tweet reason for shooting was the A.R. 15 that the Fat Boy jumped out the back of the van with, in his hand. The driver of the van threw the van in gear and stomped the gas crashing into the taxi in an attempt to flee. He caught three bullets and the passenger caught nine including two head shots which left the driver being the only one still breathing and not trying to die. By the grace of God, he made it through the gun flame and all the way to a gas station before fainting after hearing a lady scream, "Somebody call the police, he's been shot!".......

****

Now here they were in the Marriot getting ready to meet some Cuban named Carlos for the money and hopefully get a quick job that will at least make them feel better about blowing their ticket out the game.

"Who the fuck is Carlos anyway, do he got true paper cause right now his ass can get it," Re-Re said still hot about not being able to go to the beach.

"It's only one way to find out," was Kyrie's response and with that, she lead the crew out the room and towards the rental they had. Just as they walked passed the third room down the strong odor of C.F. hit their nostrils and the door swung open......

CHAPTER 21

"Malissa! come out that room girl, you been in there four days. You better not have lost your job, these bills don't pay they damn self, woman!" Malissa's mother continued to beat on the door and speak her mind regardless of her daughter's condition because she felt the girls just didn't want to grow up. It was her fault she felt, because she was now sixty-six and had Malissa at forty-five, never thought she could still get pregnant. Now she was too old to relate to the way these young kids live these days.

"Girl, you got to 1 o'clock to come out this room or else!" Although Malissa wasn't worried 'bout her old moms, she still checked her watch and it read 9:49. A.M. She then focused back to the videos and the video that was playing in her room. She'd been watching the videos she grabbed before hauling her ass out the back of the store during the murders day after day, watching and flinching off every shot. She know a lot of famous people did a lot of things they rapped about, but never believed the other part. She was now 21, brown skinned, standing at 5'5" with a model body and stripper booty and was now turned on by the gangsta shit she had witnessed her now favorite rapper do. She didn't know why she grabbed the tapes and blamed it on the movie "Menace to Society," but now she sat in her room wondering how can she reach Young Dirty without her being killed also. She also was scared as hell that the nigga she been turning down for pussy that just so happen had seen her fleeing, would come after her for seeing him bitch up. On that note, she felt the safest locked in her room which is where she stayed ....

****

Red Man had been in the hospital recovering for two weeks now and still couldn't use his left arm and had to have help using the bathroom.

"Wake up sleepy head," Shonta said from the side of his bed while lightly slappin' his face. He slowly awakened but fear took over him at the site of the silencer on the pink and chrome .380 Fat Rat bought her before his prison sentence.

"You young niggas can't do shit right. All you had to do was go in and get the money... No, you lil' mothafuckas wanna play Wild, Wild, West and now look...If I ain't know no better, I'd say you gonna tell everything when dem folks come. Cause yes nigga, they coming. Either them or the First Family and I'm not letting you talk to none of them." Without warning, one shot took his cap back and kept him sleep forever.

"When you want shit did right, you have to do the shit yourself," she said to no one because no one alive was there but her. She closed the door and walked out only to have Shay sneak in ten minutes later and discover Red Man and take a picture of his dead body. She too slid back out like she came, and hoped to find out who the fuck Shonta just killed and what did she mean by...

"If you want something done, do it yourself!"

AUTHOR BIO

Wesley Bailey Jr. is better known for his rap career, going by the name Rapper YDD. He was raised in Lake County, Florida in the city of Mount Dora (located in Central Florida north of Orlando). Reading urban novels while serving a prison sentence inspired him to make the best of his time by creating his own. Now with *Slumpvile: Slump Or Get Slumped* & *Slumpville 2: It Is What It Is* under his belt, stay tuned for more- *Slumpville 3* is most definitely on the way!

For more from Rapper YDD, go to
www.seriesbyrapperydd.com or visit his IG page
@Rapper_YDD.

$

L

U

M

P

V

I

L

L

E

2

It Is What It Is

Made in the USA
Coppell, TX
03 December 2021

67021457R00067